Seeds of Belonging

By **Dr. Danielle Hyles**   Illustrated By **Enrico Iskandar**

Seeds of Belonging

iUniverse books may be ordered through booksellers or by contacting:

iUniverse
1663 Liberty Drive
Bloomington, IN 47403
www.iuniverse.com
1-800-Authors (1-800-288-4677)

Because of the dynamic nature of the Internet, any web addresses or links contained in this book may have changed since publication and may no longer be valid. The views expressed in this work are solely those of the author and do not necessarily reflect the views of the publisher, and the publisher hereby disclaims any responsibility for them.

Any people depicted in stock imagery provided by Getty Images are models, and such images are being used for illustrative purposes only. Certain stock imagery © Getty Images.

ISBN: 978-1-6632-0355-7 (sc)
ISBN: 978-1-6632-0356-4 (e)

Library of Congress Control Number: 2020911535

Print information available on the last page.

iUniverse rev. date: 06/24/2020

Dedicated to Vivien Nicole Hyles - Dr. D.H.

At Orchard Pray Elementary School, there were many happy children in Mr. Fruits class. There was Vivien the plum; Kyra the apple; Miles the banana; Xia the orange; Deryn the grape; Troy the watermelon; Priscilla the mango; RJ the strawberry; and Elijah the pumpkin.

They loved to play, read, write and learn together in their class doing community circle time and learning in their play stations including painting, making letters out of play dough, playing in the water and sand boxes, and counting blocks.

At recess time, Vivien the plum noticed that Elijah the pumpkin was always playing by himself. She wondered why nobody would play with him.

So, Vivien the plum asked her best friend Deryn the grape to come with her to ask Elijah the pumpkin to play tag with them.

Elijah the pumpkin looked angrily at Vivien the plum and pushed Deryn the grape to the ground. Miles the banana saw what happened.

Vivien the plum and Deryn the grape told Mr. Fruits right away.

Miles the banana followed them and said, "I want to stand up for my friends.

They were bullied by Elijah the pumpkin this recess and it was not the first time."

Mr. Fruits sent Elijah the pumpkin to the school office to speak with Mrs. Vegetables, the school principal.

Principal Vegetables spoke to Elijah the pumpkin and asked him two questions. The first was, "What happened on the school yard?" and second, "How do you think you can restore your relationships with your three classmates?"

Elijah the pumpkin explained that he has felt excluded for a long time now. He feels his friends treat him differently because he believes he is a vegetable, a pumpkin that is orange and has seeds inside, and everyone else in his class is a fruit.

Elijah the pumpkin started to cry. When I moved to this school this year I just wanted to belong and fit in, but I don't. It makes me sad that I am different.

Principal Vegetables said, "My family and I are full of different kinds of vegetables and we celebrate being different. We know we bring unique gifts to our school and community."

Principal Vegetables says, "Did you know that my sister, Carrot gives nutrients to all peoples' eyes? Or my cousin, Broccoli helps all people with giving their body the iron nutrients that it needs."

Look at your family of vegetables and fruits and see all of the positive gifts they give to the community like your mother, Mrs. Salad has all kinds of healthy vegetables and fruits to share like cucumbers, melons, squash, lettuce and others that give the body lots of healthy vitamins and nutrients to protect the body from harmful diseases.

Elijah the pumpkin says to Principal Vegetables, "I never thought of it that way." And smiled at Principal Vegetables.

Principal Vegetables explained no matter if you are a fruit or a vegetable, have seeds or not, are orange or purple, come from vines or trees; you are loved by your Creator and for who you are.

Principal Vegetables called Mrs. Salad on the telephone and explained what had happened.

Mrs. Salad told her son, Elijah the pumpkin that because he has seeds inside this makes him a fruit. Elijah the pumpkin said, "Mom, all this time I taught I was a vegetable."

Mrs. Salad said, "Would that have made a difference? You are just as special, loved and gifted whether you are a vegetable or a fruit. Our differences are what make our unique gifts helpful in our community and our sameness is what gives us our family roots."

Principal Vegetables said to Elijah the pumpkin, "Now that we talked about all beauty and gifts that comes out of our sameness lets' talk about what makes us special, unique and different. You can share with your classmates what it feels like being orange, having seeds inside and being part of a family history that grows from vines." Principal Vegetables said, "Why don't you spend the rest of the afternoon with me writing about this."

So Elijah the pumpkin did. He began to write and felt the words rush into his fingertips onto the page. He was so happy to share with his classmates his "All About Me" project.

Principal Vegetables spoke to Mr. Fruits just outside her office and shared the learning that took place, and also shared as the principal that she wants all students to feel safe and cared for at school.

Principal Vegetables, Mr. Fruits and Elijah the pumpkin all sat down in the office. Elijah the pumpkin was bursting with excitement to share his "All About Me" project with Mr. Fruits.

Mr. Fruits celebrated his project and talked about how he could restore his relationships with Vivien the plum, Miles the banana and Deryn the grape.

At this point, Elijah the pumpkin was ready to apologize. He walked right up to Vivien the plum, Deryn the grape and Miles the banana in class and said, "I'm sorry, I learned from my mistake and I will not do this again."

Vivien the plum, Miles the banana and Deryn the grape
smiled with joy, and they asked Elijah the pumpkin to play tag
with them next recess, and they did.

After recess, Mr. Fruits thought it would be a good idea to share Elijah the pumpkin's "All About Me" project with the class. He was excited at first then became a little nervous.

Elijah read, "I thought I was a vegetable just like Principal Vegetables because we both grew on vines, but I discovered from my mother that I am a fruit."

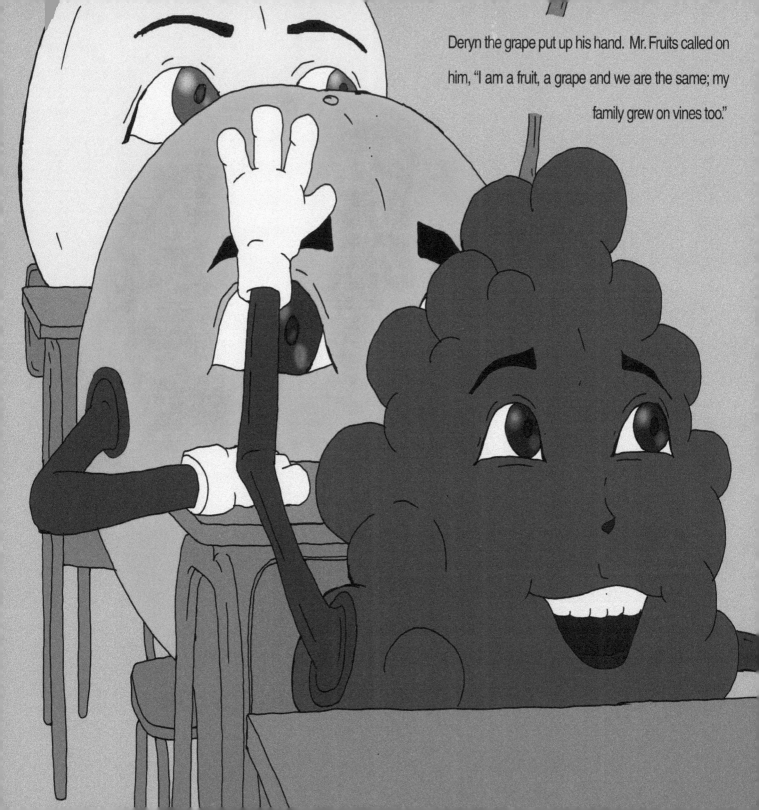

Deryn the grape put up his hand. Mr. Fruits called on him, "I am a fruit, a grape and we are the same; my family grew on vines too."

Then Elijah the pumpkin continues, "I am orange" and Xia the orange puts her hand up to speak. She says, "I am a fruit, an orange and I am the same as you. I am orange in colour too."

Elijah the pumpkin smiled and continued reading. He says, "I have seeds inside" and both Kyra the apple, and RJ the strawberry put their hands up. Kyra the apple says, "I have seeds on the inside too!" And RJ the strawberry said, "I have seeds not on the inside, but on the outside."

Troy the watermelon suddenly put his hand up. He says, "I have lots of seeds inside too." Vivien the plum and Priscillia the mango said, "We have stones." Miles the banana asks, "What is a stone?" Mr. Fruits explained, "It is one large seed."

Elijah the pumpkin turned to Mr. Fruits and said, "Thank you. I realize my classmates and I have a lot in common." Miles the banana puts his hand up and says, "One special thing about me is my skin peels. I like that, it makes me unique."

Mr. Fruits says, "Thank you Elijah the pumpkin for sharing his 'All About Me' project. We all learned a lot about the beauty of having different gifts and the sameness that makes us a loving class community."

About the Author

Dr. Danielle Hyles is a Canadian author with Trinidadian heritage who is currently a school administrator with the Durham Catholic District School Board. She has also written a research-based educational leadership book entitled "Bridging the Opportunity Gap" for educators all over the globe and a children's book called "Loving My Working Mom". Seeds of Belonging looks at bullying and how to stop it by restoring relationships and being in charge of your own actions. The fruits and vegetables in the story learn to accept how they are the same and how they are different in the family, in the class room and in the world.

CPSIA information can be obtained
at www.ICGtesting.com
Printed in the USA
BVHW012255060223
657976BV00033B/394